At Home
in a
Faraway
Place

At Home in a Faraway Place

Lynne Rae Perkins

GREENWILLOW BOOKS
An Imprint of HarperCollins*Publishers*

I would like to thank Dr. Judith M. Maxwell, Ixq'anil, of Tulane University, for her kind assistance with the Kaqchikel phrase.

At Home in a Faraway Place
Text and illustrations copyright © 2025 by Lynne Rae Perkins
All rights reserved. Manufactured in Crawfordsville, IN, United States of America.
No part of this book may be used or reproduced in any manner whatsoever without
written permission except in the case of brief quotations embodied in critical articles
and reviews. For information address HarperCollins Children's Books, a division of
HarperCollins Publishers, 195 Broadway, New York, NY 10007.
www.harpercollinschildrens.com

The text of this book is set in 12-point Berling LT Std.
The illustrations were created with some pen and ink, lots of watercolor,
and a little bit of gouache, on Arches cold press watercolor paper.
Book design by Paul Zakris

Library of Congress Cataloging-in-Publication Data

Names: Perkins, Lynne Rae, author.
Title: At home in a faraway place / written and illustrated by Lynne Rae Perkins.
Description: First edition. |
New York : Greenwillow Books, an Imprint of HarperCollins Publishers, 2025. |
Audience: Ages 8–12. | Audience: Grades 4–6. | Summary: Lissie fearlessly embraces new
experiences when she travels to Guatemala with her dad and grandmother.
Identifiers: LCCN 2024033430 (print) | LCCN 2024033431 (ebook) |
ISBN 9780063378421 (hardcover) | ISBN 9780063378452 (ebook)
Subjects: CYAC: Voyages and travels—Fiction. |
Friendship—Fiction. | Guatemala—Fiction.
Classification: LCC PZ7.P4313 At 2025 (print) | LCC PZ7.P4313 (ebook) |
DDC [Fic]—dc23
LC record available at https://lccn.loc.gov/2024033430
LC ebook record available at https://lccn.loc.gov/2024033431
24 25 26 27 28 LBC 5 4 3 2 1
First Edition

Greenwillow Books

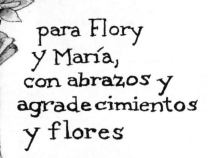

para Flory
y María,
con abrazos y
agradecimientos
y flores

for Flory
and María,
with hugs and
thanks
and flowers

1
uno

We went to a faraway place, in a different part of the world.

We went there to see Raúl, my dad's old friend from high school. My grandma came with us, because she knows Raúl too. And because she likes adventures. She is an adventurer.

It was a part of the world where most people speak Spanish. There are some kids in my school who know how to speak Spanish, but I haven't learned how yet. I asked my dad if he thought I could learn it on our trip.

"We're only going for two weeks," he said. "But you can get started. What do you know so far?"

"Not very much," I told him. It was true. I only knew a couple of words. Not enough to talk with someone.

"Well, I'm sure you'll pick up some more," said my dad.

I wondered what the place where Raúl lived would be like. My grandma and I looked at some pictures, but she had never been there either.

"So exciting!" she said. "Don't you think?"

"Uh-huh," I said.

But I was a little bit nervous. It was my first time going so far away.

2
dos

The faraway place really was far away. We flew on three different airplanes to get there. We started early in the morning, and we weren't done flying and sitting in airports until nighttime.

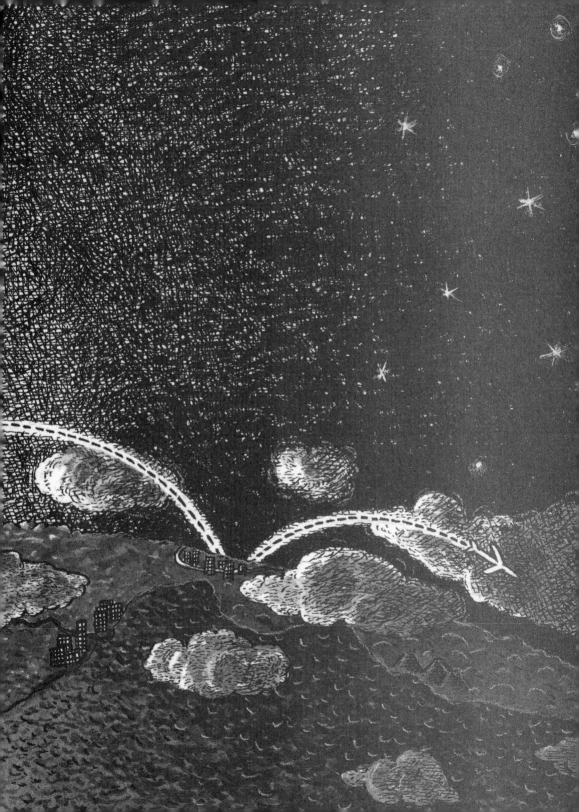

We were so tired. We stood outside the airport with crowds of people moving all around us. I wanted there to be no people. I wanted to be asleep. I held on to my grandma while my dad poked at his phone and tried to call Raúl.

And then suddenly Raúl found us, and everyone was hugging and laughing and talking. In Spanish. Even my grandma was talking in Spanish a little bit. Everyone except me.

But even I could tell when my dad was introducing me to Raúl.

"Mucho gusto," said Raúl. "It's a pleasure to meet you, Lissie."

"Mucho gusto," I said back. "It's a pleasure to meet you too."

Mucho gusto. It's a pleasure to meet you.

It didn't have the same number of words as English. But I said it anyway, and Raúl smiled, and my dad and my grandma smiled.

So I smiled too.

mucho gusto
(**moo**-choh **goo**-stoh)
it's a pleasure to meet you

3
tres

Raúl drove us through the city, full of tall buildings and bright lights and zooming cars and signs that I couldn't read.

Then the buildings were lower and farther apart, with a darkness in between them that the lights from our car could barely make a dent in.

The roads began to twist and turn. They climbed way, way up, and they dove way, way down. And back up. And back down. So there were very big hills, or even mountains, but we couldn't see them. We couldn't see anything in the pitch black of the night.

What was out there?

In the front seat, my dad and Raúl talked and talked. Sometimes in English, sometimes in Spanish. I heard my dad say my name sometimes: "Blah blah blah Lissie blah blah blah." I wondered what he was saying.

I curled up against Grandma. She put her arm around me. I leaned out of the top part of my seat belt and melted down onto her lap.

"Buenas noches, Tooty Frooty," I heard her say. She calls me that sometimes. I don't think "tooty frooty" is Spanish. But buenas noches is Spanish for good night.

buenas noches

(**bway**-nahs **noh**-chayz)

good night

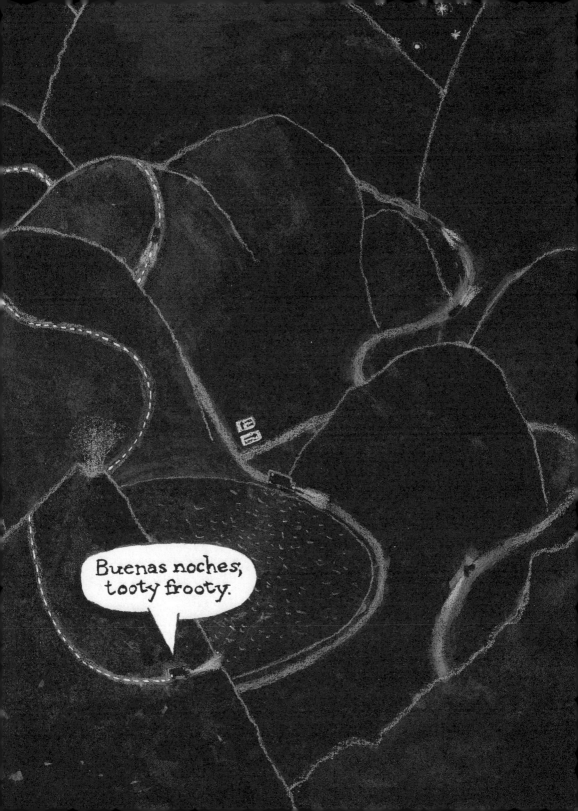

4
cuatro

I woke up in my pajamas in a soft warm bed. I couldn't remember at first where I was, or how I got there. But I could hear voices. I followed the sound of them.

I found my dad and my grandma and Raúl sitting in a little yard with a wall around it, drinking their coffee. Except for the patio where they were sitting and one little patch of grass, the yard was like a small beautiful jungle. So maybe it wasn't exactly a yard.

There were flowers, even in the trees. I thought I heard a microwave beeping, but it was a bird. I thought I heard a truck backing up, but that was another bird. Through a gap in the flowery trees, I could see a mountain with a puff of smoke coming out of the top.

"Is that a volcano?" I asked. "Is it going to explode?"

Everyone looked. Raúl laughed.

"Someday it will explode," he said. "But probably not today."

My dad and grandma laughed. I didn't laugh.

"No te preocupes," said Raúl. "Don't worry. It's not going to explode today, or even while you're here. I promise. Te lo prometo.

"Let's have some breakfast," he said.

el volcán
(vol-**kahn**, vol rhymes with bowl)
volcano

no te preocupes
(no tay pray-oh-**koo**-payz)
don't worry

grapes

juice

tortillas

eggs

salsa

plantain*

refried beans

el desayuno

(day-sigh-**you**-know)

breakfast

*kind of like bananas, fried. So good!

13

5
cinco

We saw two more volcanoes on our way into town. Only the first one was smoking. You can tell they're volcanoes because of their shape. It's like a mountain with the very top snipped off. Though sometimes the tops have clouds on them, so you can't be sure. They are just the shape you would be if you kept exploding from inside.

We walked on a skinny path alongside a road where cars and buses and motorbikes went whizzing by. Every single person we passed said, "Buenos días," which is good morning in Spanish. When we passed, somebody would have to step out into the road for a minute because there wasn't room on the path. You had to make sure no cars were coming. Or motorcycles. Or buses or trucks.

Every person said, "Buenos días," and they didn't even know us. By the time we got to the town, I could say it back. Sometimes I even said it first.

buenos días

(**bway**-nohs **dee**-ahs)

good morning

At first the town seemed to be made of walls. There were doors and windows in the walls, but they were all closed. Then the doors started to open, and we could peek in. There were beautiful gardens inside! Not in all of them, but a lot.

At home, if there is a garden, it's on the outside of the house. It made me think that maybe there are a lot of different ways to make a house.

I wanted to go into the gardens, but how did you do it? Some of them were restaurants, so you could go there if you were going to eat. But what about the ones that were inside people's houses? You might have to make friends with the people who lived there.

If you don't have friends yet, or if it's not time for lunch, you can go to a garden in a park. We went to a big one.

6
seis

It was a very historical parque.
There was a lot to say about it.

I didn't know what to say next.

chomp chomp

I knew he wasn't eating a taco. I just wanted to say a Spanish food word.

He laughed and asked me if I wanted some.

I did want some.

Something spicy was sprinkled on it.

Our hands were sticky then, so we swished them in the fountain.

Volcán. Mango. Delicioso. I was thinking maybe I actually <u>could</u> sort of speak Spanish.

I acted like an explosion, which everyone understands.

Then I made an afraid face.

I had no idea what Martín was saying. So I guess I didn't know how to speak Spanish.

But I wanted to learn.

(worm)

(flower)

(pigeon)

7
siete

In the afternoon, there are different words to say "hello." The words are "buenas tardes."

When we got back to Raúl's house, I realized that it was a door in a wall with a garden inside too. Which I was glad about, because being in a very new place can make you feel very tired, especially at first. And Raúl's garden had a hammock in it.

buenas tardes, gusano

(**bway**-nahs **tar**-dayz, goo-**sah**-no)

good afternoon, worm

buenas tardes, volcán

(**bway**-nahs **tar**-dayz, vol-**kahn**)

good afternoon, volcano

8
ocho

The next day, we actually climbed up a volcano. (So we could start off the visit with a bang, said my dad. Ha, ha.) Not the smoking one. A different one.

Grandma rode a horse because of her knees, which are not so good at steep hills. The rest of us walked, with walking sticks that some kids were selling at the bottom.

We didn't go all the way to the top. You're not allowed, because the volcano spits out lava and ashes sometimes. But we roasted marshmallows by poking our sticks into a little hollow dug into lava that was solid but still pretty hot. And we made s'mores. They were really good. I ate too many. My stomach felt funny, and I went and sat down on a rock. A very warm rock. A piece of a volcano. A volcano that could explode.

I thought my stomach might also explode. Maybe before the volcano. I put my head down. I put my elbows on my knees and closed my eyes.

Suddenly I felt a strange feeling on my hand, and I jumped. It was Grandma's horse, Rosa, licking the sticky melted marshmallow from my fingers. I turned my hand over so she could lick the other side, which was even stickier. I stood up. I forgot about my stomach.

"Buenas tardes," I said to her. Because it was afternoon. "Mucho gusto." I held out my other hand. Rosa licked that one too. I wiped my hand off on her side.

"Now we're spit sisters," I said. Her head went up and down like she was agreeing. "Yes, we're friends!"

"But I've never heard anyone say 'volcano spit,'" said Raúl later, when he told me how to say it.

"It's kind of funny, though," I said.

"It is," he said. "Chistoso."

"What?" I asked.

"Es chistoso," he said. "It's funny."

"La escupida de volcán," I said.

Raúl laughed.

"See?" I said. "It's funny!"

"Sí," said Raúl. "Es chistoso."

la escupida de caballo

(ess-koo-**pee**-dah de kah-**buy**-yo)

horse spit

la escupida de volcán

(ess-koo-**pee**-dah de vol-**kahn**)

volcano spit

es chistoso

(ess chee-**stoh**-so)

it's funny

ja, ja, ja

(ha, ha, ha)

ha, ha, ha

la cascada

(kahs-**kah**-dah)

waterfall

9

nueve

Have you ever seen a waterfall in real life? Because not everyone has. A lot of people haven't. I hadn't, but Raúl took us to two kinds of waterfalls. One was very tall and skinny, and the other one was like steps of a staircase, only the steps were pools that you could swim in.

There were some tiny brown fish in the pools that nibbled at our knees and our toes. Raúl said they only nibble at the dead skin cells, which are a normal part of skin and usually get scrubbed off when you take a bath or a shower. So it's not like the fish are eating you alive, they are just helping out. But it kind of tickles.

And Raúl said that deep down underneath the river with the pools and waterfalls, there was another river. An underground river. I tried to imagine this in my mind. It wouldn't have riverbanks and sunlight and butterflies, but it could be beautiful in its own way, whooshing along in the dark. I pictured some kind of underground creatures, like little blobs of dirt, going there for vacation. Maybe for their honeymoon. Then getting whooshed off downstream. AAAAAAHHHHHHHHHH!

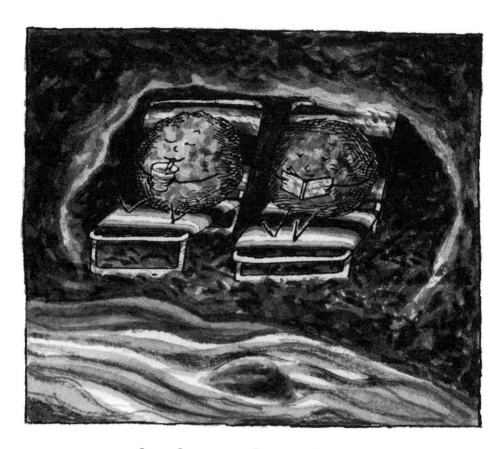

la playa subterránea
(**ply**-ah soob-teh-**rahn**-ay-ah)
underground beach

Raúl taught me how to ask what the Spanish word is for something. You can say, "¿Qué es?" That means "What is?" Or you can say, "¿Qué es esto?" That means "What is this?"

I asked him what a lot of things were, then. Maybe too many things. Because I tried to repeat everything he said, but it's hard to remember so many words all at once.

And maybe it was too many things, because my grandma said, "Whoa, Lissie, let's give poor Raúl a break."

But Raúl said, "It's all right, we're friends." Then he pointed to his nose and said, "¿Qué es esto?"

And I said, "¡La nariz!"

And he said, "¡Muy bien!" Which means "Very good!"

My favorite new word that Raúl taught me was un pez, which means a fish, but only when it's still in the water. The second it's out of the water, it's un pescado. Which is kind of easy to remember because it sounds a little bit like "pez-caught-oh."

el pez
(pehs)
fish (in the water)

el pescado

(pehs-**kah**-doh)

fish (out of the water)

10
diez

Raúl lives by himself, but he has a girlfriend named Ana. That's how I learned Spanish words about . . .

I'm only kidding. That's how I learned Spanish words for a lot of body parts, though. Because Ana has two kids, and while she taught my grandma how to make some special foods, Raúl and my dad and Flory and Mateo and I played Simon Says in Raúl's little yard.

Mostly I did whatever Raúl and Flory and Mateo were doing. But I do remember some of the words that I heard over and over again.

After Simon Says, which they called Simón dice, we walked to a dusty field down the street. Cars and motorbikes zoomed past it on two sides. A couple of dogs sniffed the edges, maybe looking for food or rabbits or something. And on the far side of the field, some kids were kicking around a ball. When they saw us, they started to leave.

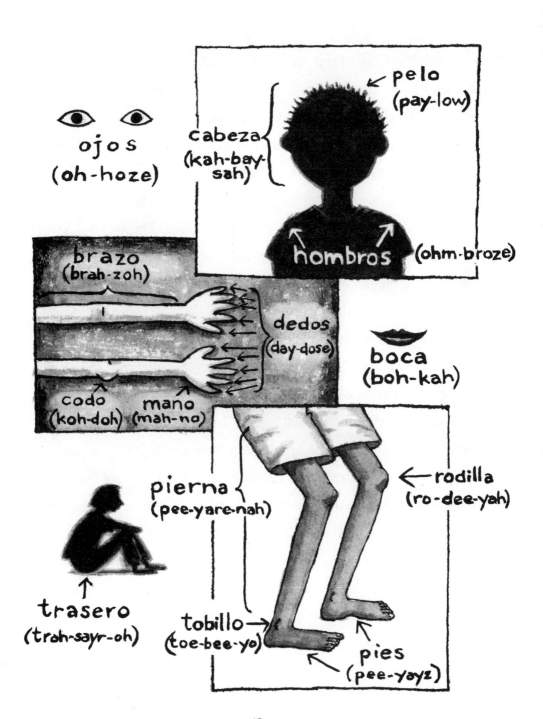

ojos
(oh-hoze)

pelo
(pay-low)

cabeza
(kah-bay-sah)

hombros (ohm-broze)

brazo
(brah-zoh)

dedos
(day-dose)

boca
(boh-kah)

codo
(koh-doh)

mano
(mah-no)

pierna
(pee-yare-nah)

rodilla
(ro-dee-yah)

trasero
(trah-sayr-oh)

tobillo
(toe-bee-yo)

pies
(pee-yayz)

43

Then Raúl called out to them. I don't know what he said, but before I knew it, we were all playing soccer together. So probably he said, "Hey, you wanna play some soccer with us?"

The Spanish word for soccer is fútbol. Which makes sense, when you think about it. And here is a great thing about soccer: you can do it without talking very much. You can pass someone the ball. Or you can get in a good position and wave your arms. You can clap and jump around when your team scores, or when your goalie blocks a shot.

There are a million things you can do, and everyone knows what they mean. Even if you just shout or groan, everyone gets it, because it sounds happy or excited or disappointed. Or it can sound like shrieks of agony.

That's the type of sound I guess I made when I was running backward and went to turn and somehow got my feet tangled up together and I twisted my ankle and fell flat on my back and bonked my head on the ground and lay there like a sack of concrete. Everything was swirling all around me.

The boy named Vicente was there in a flash, helping me to sit up. I could tell that with his eyes, he was asking me, "Are you okay?"

But I didn't know yet if I was okay or not.

Then my dad was helping me over to a sort of wooden box I could sit on, and he sat beside me and put his arm around me and asked me questions and looked at my head and my ankle and asked could I move my foot (I could), and then into my eyeballs, because I guess that is very important when you bonk your head.

I leaned against him. I wasn't really paying attention to the game, but the others were still playing, at least for a while.

When I started to feel better, I looked up and saw that no one was left on the field.

"Where did they all go?" I asked.

My dad pointed across the street. Raúl and all the kids were standing at a counter outside a little store. They turned and waited for an empty space in the traffic, then they swarmed back over to the field. Everyone had Popsicles. Everyone but us.

I looked at my dad. He probably didn't care, but I did. He gave a little sideways nod, and his eyes looked to that side, which meant I was supposed to look there too. So I did, and I saw Flory and Vicente coming toward us, eating Popsicles, but also carrying Popsicles for Dad and me. Flory gave one to Dad and skittered away.

Vicente handed me the other one. It was orange. He smiled.

"You are okay?" he asked.

"Yeah," I said. "Sí." I pointed to my head. "Mi cabeza es bueno. Gracias."

I know I wasn't saying it quite right. But he could tell what I meant.

"Bueno," he said.

I slurped the melty part from the Popsicle.

"Mmm," I said. "Delicioso."

Vicente slurped the melty part from his Popsicle. He pointed at my ankle and said, "¿Y el tobillo?"

My dad said, "He's asking about your—"

"I know, I know, I know!" I interrupted him.

"Tobillo es bueno," I said to Vicente. "Gracias."

I was running out of things I could say, but I wanted to keep talking. So I pointed at my Popsicle and said, "¿Qué es esto? ¿Por favor?"

"Es una paleta," said Vicente. "Una paleta de hielo."

I was confused. I pointed at the soccer ball that was whizzing through the air behind him and said, "¿Paleta?"

He turned to see, and then laughed. He pointed at the ball and said, "La pelota." He held up the Popsicle and said, "La paleta." He pointed at each thing again. "Pelota. Paleta."

I repeated it after him. Pelota. Paleta. Pelota. Paleta. Pelota. Paleta.

We were kind of done with our paletas now. Vicente pointed at the field where the other kids and Raúl were playing again and said, "¿Quieres jugar?" I could tell it meant, "Do you want to play?" So I said, "Sí."

Because I did.

So for the rest of the tarde, we kicked the pelota and ran and fell down and got up and ran again. The dogs watched us from the edge of the field as if they watched fútbol games all the time. The cars and the motorbikes and the buses whizzed and rumbled by, but it was just a noise, like rain on the roof. When the sun went down behind the tallest trees, it was time to go home, and we said adiós and other goodbye words (I guess) to the kids we had played with: Vicente and Miguel and Eliseo and Chofo.

la pelota
(pay-**loh**-tah)
ball

la paleta

(pah-**lay**-tah)

Popsicle

11
once

Back at Raúl's house, we had to wash off the dirt from the dusty field. Which was dusty because it was the dry season. We washed our manos, our brazos, our piernas, and our caras. And we put on clean camisetas.

When we were clean as whistles (that's English, but what does it even mean?), it was time for dinner. Which we ate on the roof! It was flat, and there were stairs that went up to it, and there was a table there, and chairs. The sky was all around, and when it got dark we lit candles. One of the volcanoes glowed a little at the top. No te preocupes, though.

Ana and Grandma had made different kinds of food, but the most delicious one was a sort of brown stew with chicken in it, and rice.

There was a couch on the roof, with a blanket, and after we ate, Flory and Mateo and I wrapped ourselves up in it. It was getting chilly. Flory was a little bit older than me, and Mateo was younger.

He fell asleep almost right away. We all snuggled while the grown-ups talked and talked.

They were telling stories in Spanish and in English so that Grandma and Ana could both understand. Because Grandma knew some Spanish and Ana knew some English, but they didn't speak as easily as Dad and Raúl. So Flory and I could mostly understand too. We got the idea.

There was a story with an earthquake in it, and running out of a house. (From Ana, when she was little.)

There was a story with a flood, and floating down a street in a rowboat. (Grandma.)

There were stories about taking vegetables to market very early in the morning, when it was really still night. (Ana and Grandma.)

There was a story about getting lost in the woods on a hiking trip and only having three Pop-Tarts to eat and no tent or sleeping bags. (Dad and Raúl.)

There were a lot of stories. So many stories. There were so many stars in the sky. The top of that one volcano glowed, but just barely. Like a night-light.

Flory and I scrunched up under the blanket at different ends of the little couch. Mateo nestled between us, his head tilted back onto the cushion and his knees pulled up in a blankety mound. His mouth was partly open. He reminded me of a puppy. Although I guess puppies don't pull up their knees or sleep with their mouths open. (Or do they?)

Anyway, just then, a leaf drifted down out of the darkness and landed exactly on his forehead. Flory saw it too. We looked at each other and smiled. Then we looked back at Mateo, to see if he would wake up. But he didn't.

Flory slowly reached over and plucked the leaf by its curled-up stem. She held it in the air, watching Mateo's face, then set it back down, but on his nose. We watched, waiting. A frown flitted across his face, but he didn't move.

I carefully lifted the leaf from his nose and put it between his nose and his mouth, like a mustache. His nose twitched once. The leaf fluttered when he breathed out. Flory moved the leaf to his chin. Then she pulled the elastic from the end of one of her braids, shook it out, and flipped it toward her brother's face, sort of like gently throwing a frisbee. I guessed that she was aiming for his nose, like ring toss, but she overshot. The hair tie landed on the cheek closest to me.

"¿La nariz?" I asked softly.

She nodded, and put her hand on her mouth to keep from laughing.

Like in pick-up sticks, my hand moved in slow motion toward the hair tie. One part was raised up from Mateo's cheek, so I grasped that between my finger and my thumb with super precision and raised it into the air. I held it over Mateo's nariz and dropped it. Which should have worked, but all of a sudden he turned to one side, still sleeping, and curled into a ball. The hair tie landed on his cheek and slid off.

Flory and I looked at each other.

"Rats," I said. She smiled.

"Oh well," she said. It was the first time I heard her say English words.

"Do you speak English?" I asked.

Flory held her thumb and her first finger about a half inch apart.

"Solo un poco," she said. "Just a little."

"Solo un poco," I repeated. "Solo un poco español," I said, pointing to myself.

The grown-ups were still talking, but softer, and the words seemed farther apart. The sky was still full of stars. It was cozy under the blanket. My eyes might have closed for a little while.

But before I forget, the Spanish word for love is amor.

And the Spanish words for "Good night, my love" are "Buenas noches, mi amor."

Which can be the same whether you are talking about mushy love, or whether it's your grandma tucking your blanket around you.

buenas noches, mi amor

(**bway**-nahs **noh**-chayz, mee ah-**mor**)

good night, my love

12
doce

One day Flory and I played the game where you draw a cabeza at the top and fold the paper at the neck. Then the other person draws the next part of the body without being able to see what kind of cabeza it is, and folds the paper again. Then after someone draws los pies, you open it up and it's a hodge-podge creature.

Flory drew excellent wings, which are called alas. And frog legs, which are patas de rana. Her frog legs were very muscly, like a superhero.

Maybe you are thinking, "But I thought legs were piernas?" That is if they are human legs. Animal legs are patas.

We drew some patas and some alas. And some other things.

frog legs
patas de rana

patas de gato
cat legs

dog legs

patas de perro

patas de araña
spider legs

patas de caballo
horse legs

chicken legs
patas de pollo

horse's head

cabeza de caballo

cabeza de pollo

chicken head

alas de pollo
chicken wings

horse wings
alas de caballo

also chicken wings

alitas de pollo

barriga
tummy

I knew I wouldn't remember all of the words. Not right away. And Flory would probably not remember all of the English words right away. But we can look at our drawings.

Once he woke up from his nap, Mateo made a drawing too. He spent a long time on it. It was really good. There was a lot happening: ninjas and eagles and explosions.

At bedtime that night, I talked with my dad.

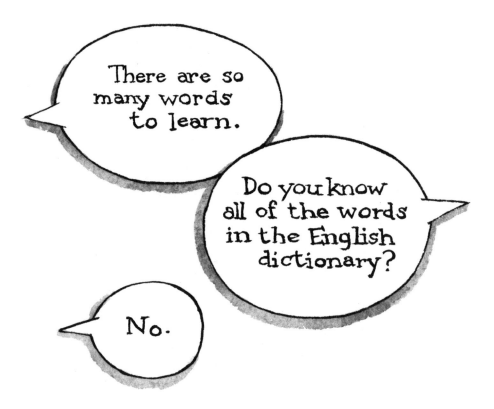

There are so many words to learn.

Do you know all of the words in the English dictionary?

No.

Can we still talk to each other?

Yes.

So, you don't have to know ALL the words.

Okay. Buenas noches.

Buenas noches, honey pie.

13
trece

Flory and I both knew how to make friendship bracelets. But we showed each other different kinds.

I made mine fast. But Flory made hers perfect. I tried to slow down so I could make a perfect one for her from me. And she speeded up to make one as fast as me. Which she could, no problem. But she liked making perfect ones better.

We made so many! We piled them in the middle of the table, even the ones that Mateo made that basically had one knot in them. Then all three of us took turns closing our eyes and picking one to put on. You had to put on the first one you touched. We put them on both arms. They looked very beautiful.

las pulseras de la amistad
(pool-**sayr**-ahs day lah ah-mee-**stahd**)
friendship bracelets

14
catorce

Sometimes at home I sit out in the backyard at night with my dad and my grandma, or with my friends. We find the Big Dipper, and Cassiopeia, which looks like a W, though it's supposed to be a lady sitting in a chair.

But people in the very olden days looked at the sky way more than most of us do. They paid attention to how stars moved across the sky, and where and when the sun rose and set. They figured out exactly how many days are in a year just by looking and noticing and keeping track. They also figured out eclipses.

Some of the olden-days people used what they noticed to build buildings where sunlight might come in through a small hole and light up a room only two times a year. Or they might build a pyramid where, if you stood on top of it on certain days, the sun would rise exactly over certain other buildings. It helped them keep track of seasons for farming, because otherwise the rainy season, which is good for crops, could sneak up on you and take you by surprise.

We went to see one of the pyramid places, but not on one of the special days, and not at sunrise. The pyramids were big and made of stone, with steps going all the way up. The people who built them were called Mayans, and they did it, like, a thousand years ago. And all by hand, without machines.

"Can you imagine?" asked my grandma. She sat down on a low stone wall and looked around. "I have wanted to see these all my life," she said. "In person, I mean. I can't believe I'm actually here."

I sat down beside her. I looked around too. I knew I was supposed to feel lucky and amazed, but I mostly felt hot. Also, I was wishing Flory was there, but it was a school day.

"Did the olden-days people have swimming pools?" I asked.

Grandma handed me her water bottle and said, "Here. Drink some water. You'll feel better."

And I did, a little bit.

"These pyramids would be good for playing Stone School," I said. (Which, if you don't know, is a game where you go up and down steps depending on whether you guess which hand someone is holding a stone in.)

Grandma laughed. "They would," she said, "but I don't think ordinary people could go up the steps. I think only priests and royalty were allowed."

"But don't you think you would want to, if no one was looking?" I asked.

"They are tempting," said Grandma. "But they're sacred too. It would be disrespectful. And the penalties might have been harsh."

Grandma had studied up. And Raúl knew a lot too. But neither of them knew as much as the guide, Luis. He told us so, so many things. Here is what I remember.

He told us how the stone carvings tell stories, but you have to know how to read them. Like, if a person is standing on top of another person, it doesn't mean they actually stood on them (though, maybe). It means they had defeated them, or took them captive or something. Everything tells part of the story, like who it was and when it happened.

Luis told us that the Mayans **zero** might have been the first people in the world to have **one** the idea of zero in their math. Which is important **five** because it's how we tell 1 from 10. They also had writing, and books.

People didn't live in the pyramids. Important people were sometimes buried in them, and they were used for ceremonies. Only the priests and the royalty went to the top. (Grandma was right.) But the big open areas would be filled with people. I tried to imagine that. It was empty and quiet when we were there.

Luis showed us how if you clap your hands, the sound echoes back from all the steps of the pyramid at a slightly different time, and the echoes blur together to sound like the call of a bird—the quetzal, a beautiful bird with bright colors. And a very long tail.

There was a ball court made of stone. The ball was solid rubber, not rubber filled with air, and you had to hit it with parts of your body other than your hands and feet. You could get all bruised up, so the players wore padding. And fancy headdresses. But probably not this fancy.

Luis told us so many things, and I can't remember them all. And I am probably remembering some of them wrong.

Like about a Mayan belief that when a person is born, they are connected to a certain animal or part of nature, and they are like that animal somehow. People think in different ways about how it works, but maybe for example a warrior was a person but could also be somehow connected to a jaguar.

I asked my dad if he thought this was true. He said, "There are a lot of ideas in the world, and it doesn't hurt to think about them. This one makes me remember that we are animals too. Everything in nature is connected, and we don't always understand how."

It was such a Dad answer.

But I thought about the time when a fox and her kit were living in a drainage pipe in front of our house. They would come out and play, right in the street. And once when I was walking home from my friend's house, they didn't run back into the pipe, they just sat there and looked at me like I was their neighbor stopping by for a visit. I looked back. We were connected with our eyes for almost a minute.

I had felt a little bit like a fox then. I'd felt a little bit wild. So maybe it's like that. Or maybe not.

"The Spanish word for fox," said Raúl, "is zorro for a male, and zorra for a female."

la zorra

(zorr-ah)

female fox

We were allowed to go to the top of one pyramid by walking up wooden steps, so we wouldn't wear out the stones. They didn't look like they would ever wear out, but I guess they can. They *are* called ruins.

We weren't the only ones up there. People were taking pictures of themselves and each other and the view, which was treetops forever. But people came and went, and there was a little time when it was just Luis and Grandma and me. I could tell by Grandma's face that she was having a "peak experience," which is her expression for having a really good time. She does it a lot.

"It's a whole other world," she said, peering through the trees at all the stone buildings full of steps, around us and below us. "There are so many worlds, aren't there?"

Luis laughed. "Cada cabeza es un mundo," he said.

Grandma's lips moved as she figured that out in her head. "Every head is a world?" she said.

"Yes," said Luis. "Like, everyone has their own whole world inside their head."

"Oh, that's true, isn't it?" said Grandma. "But I'm thinking of this whole world of people who just disappeared."

"We're not gone," said Luis. "We don't build pyramids anymore, but we're still here."

Grandma kind of slapped herself on the forehead, as if she knew

she'd said something stupid. "Of course." She smiled. "Although I still wish I could visit those other times, just for a little while."

"This might be as close as we can get," said Luis. "But just imagine . . ."

He was talking to me now. "Look at this little lizard."

We squatted down to look at a lizard that was soaking up all of the sun.

"Someone a thousand years ago probably looked at a lizard just like this on this very same rock. That's kind of like time travel."

In my mind, just for a second, I was someone a thousand years ago, looking at a lizard on a rock in the sun. Then I was back.

"What would I say to the lizard a thousand years ago?" I asked.

"Hmmm," said Luis. "Maybe something like, 'How's it going, little lizard?' In Spanish, that's '¿Qué tal, lagartija?' But a thousand years ago, the Spanish weren't here yet. So maybe you could say, 'La ütz awäch, ti spach?'"

I tried saying it. It took a few tries. "Are those real words?" I asked.

Luis nodded. "It's Kaqchikel," he said. "One of the languages people spoke back then, though maybe not at this particular place. And people still speak it. It was the first language I learned."

"How many languages do you know?" I asked.

"Just three," he said.

"That's a lot!" I said. "I only know one."

"But you're learning, right?" he said.

"Sí," I said.

"Eso es bueno," he said.

The little lizard wandered off in its lizardy way and disappeared over the edge of one of the huge stones. I started to go see where it was going, but when I looked down and saw how high up we were, my knees got wobbly and I had to sit down.

"Adiós, lagartija," I said.

la ütz awäch, ti spach

(lah ootz ah-**wetch**, tee spahtch)

'how's it going, little lizard' in Kaqchikel

15
quince

I showed Flory the pictures of the ruins on my grandma's phone. Then I showed her some other pictures of our casa and our perro and of me with my friends.

"¿Dónde está tu mamá?" she asked.

"Dónde está" means "where is."

I thought for a minute. I went to the notes part of my Grandma's phone and drew with my finger.

I drew a red line in between my dad and me, and my mom and Greg. There's not a red line in real life, and everyone is nice to each other, but it kind of explains it. Also, my mom and I don't usually wear skirts, but, you know.

"¿Dónde está tu papá?" I asked. I was kind of afraid to ask, but she had asked about my mom.

Flory thought for a second. She pointed to Greg in my drawing and said, "Mi papá." And pointed at the woman and said, "Marisela." Then she said, "Son divorciados."

So I learned those words too.

I found a picture on the phone of my mom and Greg and me, and showed it to her. Then she went and got Ana's phone and showed me pictures from their life: their casa, their gato, her amigas and familia, her papá and Marisela.

Then we used the phones to play Minecraft.

qué quieres hacer

(kay kee-**ayr**-ays ah-**sayr**)

what do you want to do

16
dieciséis

Here is a useful question that Flory and I learned to ask each other:
What do you want to do? Or in Spanish, ¿Qué quieres hacer?
And then you can say words you both know.

Or you can act things out.

And then you can say another useful thing, which is "No sé, ¿qué quieres hacer *tú*?" Which is the same as, "I don't know, what do *you* want to do?"

no sé, qué quieres hacer tú

(no say, kay kee-**ayr**-ays ah-**sayr** too)

I don't know, what do you want to do

17
diecisiete

Some days, Raúl took us to turista places, places where tourists go. Because that's what my dad and my grandma and I were. And because they were interesting places to go.

Like a big church that had mostly crumbled in an earthquake a long time ago. The roof was gone, so you could see the sky from inside. There were angels on the walls and it felt all peaceful and holy, even the cat that watched us walk around.

pod

Many steps. But you can do it!

us

We went to a place where we learned how to make chocolate out of cacao beans, which grow on trees. And we drank a thick warm chocolatey drink.

We climbed a very big hill. From the top of it, we could see the whole town, and the mountains (and volcanoes) all around. Raúl showed us where his house was.

While we were walking around, we saw the most amazing-looking buses I have ever seen. They were painted in super-bright colors, including pictures of people's faces and words in fancy letters. Some had little lights on the outside and music blasting from inside. And we saw tiny taxis with three wheels, like a combination of a car and a tricycle. These are called tuc tucs. We rode in both things.

ROSALITA

Some days we went to everyday kinds of places, like the grocery store, or to play fútbol, or just to walk around or sit in the parque and watch the pigeons. I liked those days, because I started to feel at home. I knew where to go, and how to ask for one empanada, please. Or two. They are little pies you can hold in your hand, with chicken or other stuff inside.

The lady who sold empanadas recognized me and asked me how I was. And I said I was fine, thank you, and how was she?

The mercado is a place where turistas go, but also an everyday place. Everyone goes there, because it's a market with every kind of food, and every kind of everything. Because mercado means market.

I could eat one million chiles rellenos. I don't know what they are exactly, but they are fried and they are delicious.

We were eating chiles rellenos when someone called my name. I didn't even notice at first, because I didn't expect anyone there to know me. And also, it didn't quite sound like my name. But Flory grabbed my arm and pointed to a boy who was sitting in the next booth over. He smiled and waved, and said, "Hola, Lissie." Then he pointed to himself and said, "Martín." He was the boy from the first day in the parque!

I didn't know enough words to explain this to Flory, but I guess that's what Martín told her. They talked very fast, and laughed. Their words rushed by my ears like cars on a superhighway. Like racehorses. Like water from a faucet. I tried to recognize words, but I could only hear a few. Like, volcán.

I felt lost in all those words, like I would never understand. Until Flory put her arm around my waist and said, "Somos amigas."

Then Martín said, "Somos amigos, también."

I knew exactly what they were saying.

"Sí, somos amigos," I said. "¿Qué quieres hacer?"

somos amigos
(**soh**-mohs ah-**mee**-gohs)
we are friends
(male, or both male and female)

18
dieciocho

That night at Raúl's house, I told him about all those words flying by me so fast, and how I couldn't understand any of them.

"I know exactly how you felt," said Raúl. "I felt the same way when I first came to your country and went to school with your dad. But bit by bit, you learn. Let's practice rolling your Rs."

"Rolling my what?" I asked.

"Your Rs," said Raúl. And then he showed me how you say Rs in Spanish, by sort of flicking your tongue on the roof of your mouth.

Sometimes just once, and it sounds like the Ts in "butter." So "Flory" sounds kind of like "Flo-dy."

And sometimes more than once, which sounds like when people imitate the noise a motorcycle makes. So we practiced making motorcycle sounds.

And we practiced saying his name: R-R-R-aúl. It sounded really funny. But also cool.

"Es chistoso, ¿no?" he asked.

"Sí," I said. "Es chistoso."

"See?" he said. "You know stuff."

R-R-R-R-R-R-R-R

(D-D-D-D-D-D-D-D)

the sound of rolling Rs

19
diecinueve

Which animals are wild? Which animals are tame? Which ones are in between? It can be different in different places in the world.

My dad says he has been to a beach where wild pigs swim in the ocean, right alongside the humans. And the fish.

There are people who train pigeons to deliver messages. And some cats would rather live outside than inside a house. Horses can be wild or tame.

There are places where dogs, some of them, live outside on their own. In little groups, usually of three or four. The town where Raúl and Flory and Ana and Mateo live has some of these dogs. They don't bother you or bark at you, they just glance as you go by. Like pigeons or squirrels, but bigger. And you should leave them alone, because they probably haven't been to the veterinarian lately. But some people put food and water out for them.

We talked about all this, about animals and wildness and tameness, one day while we were eating lunch from a food cart in town. Because I had asked Raúl about the dogs.

"Are there dogs here who do live in houses?" I asked. "With people?"

"Yes," he said. "Of course."

And then he taught me a very fun thing about Spanish words. You can put "ito" at the end of some words, and it means the same thing, but smaller. So perro means dog, and perrito means small dog.

And perritito means even smaller dog.

And perrititito means a *really* small dog.

It's not foolproof, though. A burrito can be a small burro, or it can be something to eat.

Our lunch was pupusas, another kind of bread with stuff inside. I put a little bit of mine into my pocket. When we passed one of the corners where some dogs were hanging out, I saw Raúl bend down and set something on the ground by a pan of water that was sitting there. It was a piece of his pupusa. So I put my bit down next to his. It would be a nice snack for them.

el perro
(**pair**-oh)
dog

el perrito
(payr-**ee**-toh)
small dog

el perritito
(payr-ee-**tee**-toh)
wee little dog

el perrititito
(payr-ee-tee-**tee**-toh)
super small dog

It also works for cats:

el gato
(**gah**-toh)
cat

el gatito
(gah-**tee**-toh)
small cat

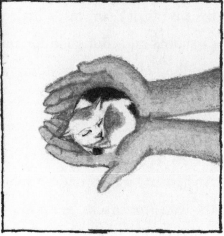

el gatitito
(gah-tee-**tee**-toh)
wee little cat

el gatititito
(gah-tee-tee-**tee**-toh)
super small cat

20
veinte

Our trip was almost over. We drove, all of us, to a beach on the ocean. The sand was black, because it was made of volcano lava that burst into a zillion teeny-tiny pieces the minute it hit the ocean water. And it was hot, because black soaks up warmth from the sun. We had to wear flip-flops when we walked on it. I had to put on sunblock of SPF one thousand because the sun was so bright.

Raúl and my dad went in the ocean on surfboards. And this might sound crazy, but even though we were right there at the ocean, the rest of us hung out at the swimming pool of the hotel. Because the ocean was "a little too exciting" that day. That's what Grandma said. But good for surfing. We could see Dad and Raúl paddling out and then riding the waves back in. We could hear their faint shouts.

At the pool, we played keep-away. We jumped off the diving board. We floated. We did every beautiful thing that pools are for. And we ate snacks under umbrellas. Raúl and Dad came in from the water for snacks. For fuel.

A little feeling in the back of my head got bigger as the day went by. It was the feeling of goodbye. I felt like I needed to say something, something I didn't know how to say. I asked Grandma for help. She had to think about it, then she taught me to say it. It was long and complicated, with new words, so we practiced. I wrote it down on a piece of paper, in case I got nervous and forgot.

We were leaving at night. Raúl was driving us to the airport, but it was going to be late, so Ana and Mateo and Flory were staying at the hotel.

We ate dinner, all of us, at a table on the beach under a shelter with a roof made of palm leaves. The sun set over the ocean, and just before it went down, it lit up everyone's face, rosy and golden and magical. Even when the sun was gone, the sky was still beautiful with clouds that changed colors every minute, until they were almost the same blue-purple-gray as the sky. We had a candle on our table now, in a glass jar. I felt like time was slipping away.

"¿Qué quieres hacer?" I asked Flory.

She pointed to the ocean. We looked at Grandma and Ana, and they nodded.

"Be careful, though," said Grandma.

The sand was still warm, but you could walk on it barefoot now. We walked to the edge of the water and let it rush over our feet and ankles. It wasn't even that cold.

There was just a little light left. I pulled my piece of paper out of my pocket and whispered the words one more time. Then I looked up at Flory and said them out loud.

estoy feliz de conocerte
(ess-**toy** fay-**lees** day koh-no-**sayr**-tay)
I'm happy to know you

"Estoy feliz de conocerte," I said. "Espero que nos volvamos a ver."

Flory smiled a big smile. Then she held up her own piece of paper and wiggled it.

espero que nos volvamos a ver

(ess-**payr**-oh kay nohs vol-**vah**-mohs ah vayr)

I hope we see each other again

"I'm happy to know you," she said. "I hope we see each other again."

Which is the exact same thing that I said!

I smiled too. A very big smile. And then we hugged.

sonrisas

(sohn-**ree**-sahs)

smiles

abrazos

(ah-**brah**-sohs)

hugs

21
veintiuno

The airport was crowded with people: hurrying, waiting in lines, talking. The talking was like a word search puzzle that you listen to.

I was more used to this feeling now. I listened for the words I knew and let the rest go by, like catching fish (¡pescados!) in a net. I have never actually done that, but I can imagine it.

We shuffled through the long back-and-forth lines where they look at your passport. We walked past stores of souvenirs and T-shirts and snacks. When we got to our gate, the seats were already nearly filled up, even though there were a lot of them. We finally found three together across from a mother with two kids and a baby. The baby was mad about something, and the mother jiggled it and cooed to it. She stood up and held the baby to her shoulder and walked in circles.

The two kids, a girl and a boy, started fussing at each other, and the mom said something to them that must have meant "Settle down!" Which they did, for a minute or two. Then they started fussing again. The baby was still wailing. The mom cradled the baby in her arms and danced around.

"That poor woman," said my grandma. "Traveling with three

little ones, and so late at night."

The two kids were out of their seats now, giving each other pushes.

"Hey!" I said. They turned and looked at me.

"¿Quieres jugar Simón dice?" I asked.

They looked confused. Maybe I said it wrong. Or maybe they didn't know what Simon Says was. I put my hands on my head and said, "Simón dice toca la cabeza."

They toca-ed their cabezas. I stood up.

"Simón dice toca los pies." They toca-ed their pies.

We did all the body parts I could remember. So I acted out things that I didn't know the words for, like "jump up and down" and "spin around." Then we started over. Halfway through the second round, I noticed that Grandma was sitting with the mom. She was tickling the baby's barriga. She was saying sweet things. The baby laughed. The mom smiled.

The girl tapped my arm.

"Me gustan tus pulseras," she said. I looked down. I still had all those friendship bracelets on each arm. I worked one off over my hand and gave it to her.

Her brother said, "A mí me gustan las pulseras también." So I gave him one too.

"¿Somos amigos?" I asked.

"Sí," they said, both at once. "Somos amigos."

It was late. I didn't know how to say, "Simon Says let's all sit down and relax." But I just sat down on the carpeted floor, and they did too. I pointed to myself and said, "Lissie."

"¿No eres Simón?" asked the boy.

"No," I shook my head. "Lissie."

Their names were Emilia and Rubén. The baby was calm now, maybe asleep. Their mom fished around in her backpack and found a coloring book and some crayons. Emilia and Rubén and I sat there and colored, with the announcements from the loudspeakers blaring around us.

The announcement for their group came before ours, so they gathered themselves up and we waved goodbye. But before they left, Rubén tore out one of the pictures we had been coloring and gave it to me. It was dinosaurs of every color. Which could be accurate, who knows?

"Gracias," I said. "¡Adiós!"

"¡Adiós!" he said.

And then he said something I didn't understand.

But someday, I will.

los amigos dinosaurios con pulseras

(ah-**mee**-gose dee-no-**sow**-ree-ohs cone pool-**sayr**-ahs)

dinosaur friends with bracelets

22
veintidós

On the airplane, I told Grandma about the bracelets.

"I know it's not a real friendship," I said. "We probably won't ever see them again. But it felt like a tiny one."

"Tiny friendships are real too," said Grandma. "The world is held together by tiny friendships. And bigger ones too, of course. That's what I think, anyway."

"I think the one with Flory could be a bigger one," I said.

"I think so too," said Grandma. "I think it very well could be."

I leaned on her shoulder. My dad took the airplane blanket out of its plastic bag and tucked it around me. He held my hand while the airplane revved its motors, zoomed down the runway, and lifted us up into the night, flying like a bird, a giant bird, going home.

"Hasta luego, volcanes," I said to myself. But hasta luego is not goodbye. It means "See you later."

"Hasta luego, perrititos. Hasta luego, amigos. Espero que nos volvamos a ver."

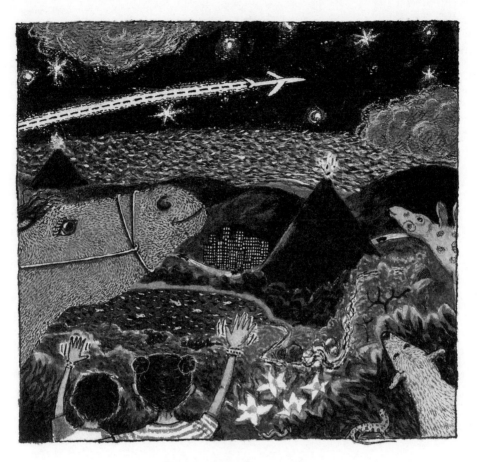

hasta luego
(**ah**-stah loo-**way**-go)
see you later

Author's Note

I have been studying Spanish for a few years now. I still have a ways to go. But I'm learning. One of my favorite feelings ever is when my teacher, who is Guatemalan, tells me stories in Spanish about her childhood or her life now, and I can follow what she's saying. Another is when we are talking and a string of Spanish words pours out of my mouth, and they even make sense. I love how these things feel in my brain. I love hearing stories about a life in some ways quite unlike my own, but in other ways, important ways, very much the same. And I love that we are two people from faraway worlds, getting to know each other.

I can be a shy traveler, but what I like best about any adventure is connecting with people: a conversation, a shared experience, a kindness, a laugh. A tiny friendship. We can find ways to connect without speaking the same language. But it's really fun to try to learn one. And friendships, even tiny ones, are what hold the world together.

Spanish words and phrases that Lissie learned

los abrazos / (ah-**brah**-zohs) / hugs

las alas / (**ah**-lahs) / wings

las alitas / (ah-**lee**-tahs) / little wings

las amigas / (ah-**mee**-gahs) / friends, female

los amigos / (ah-**mee**-gohs) /
  friends, male, or both male and female

la araña / (ah-**rah**-nyah) / spider

la barriga / (bah-**ree**-gah) / tummy

la boca / (**boh**-kah) / mouth

el brazo / (**brah**-zoh) / arm

buenos días / (**bway**-nohs **dee**-ahs) / good morning

buenas noches / (**bway**-nahs **no**-chayz) / good night

buenas noches, mi amor / (**bway**-nahs **noh**-chayz, mee ah-**mor**) /
  good night, my love

buenas tardes, gusano / (**bway**-nahs **tar**-dayz, goo-**sah**-no) /
good afternoon, worm

buenas tardes, volcán / (**bway**-nahs **tar**-dayz, vol-**kahn**) /
good afternoon, volcano

la cabeza / (kah-**bay**-sah) / head

cada cabeza es un mundo / (**kah**-dah kah-**bay**-sah es oon **moon**-doh) /
every head is a world

las camisetas / (kah-mee-**seh**-tahs) / T-shirts

la cascada / (kahs-**kah**-dah) / waterfall

los chiles rellenos / (**chee**-lays ray-**yay**-nohs) /
stuffed chile peppers, fried

el codo / (**koh**-doh) / elbow

cómo está / (**koh**-moh ess-**tah**) / how are you (more formal)

cómo estás / (**koh**-moh ess-**tahs**) / how are you (more familiar)

de / (day) / of

del, or de la / (dell, or day lah) / also both mean "of"

los dedos / (**day**-dohs) / fingers or toes

delicioso / (deh-lee-see-**oh**-so) / delicious

divorciados / (dee-vor-see-**ah**-dohs) / divorced (plural)

dónde está / (**dohn**-day ess-**tah**) / where is

la empanada / (em-pah-**nah**-dah) / hand-pie with savory filling

es chistoso / (ess chee-**stoh**-so) / it's funny

la escupida de caballo / (ess-koo-**pee**-dah de kah-**buy**-yo) /
    horse spit

la escupida de volcán / (ess-koo-**pee**-dah de vol-**kahn**) / volcano spit

espero que nos volvamos a ver /
    (ess-**payr**-oh kay nohs vol-**vah**-mohs ah vayr) /
    I hope we see each other again

está bien / (ess-**tah** bien) / it's okay, it's fine

estoy feliz de conocerte / (ess-**toy** fay-**lees** day koh-no-**sayr**-tay) /
I'm happy to know you

la flor / (floor) / flower

el fútbol / (**foot**-bowl, foot rhymes with shoot) / soccer (in the USA)

la gallina / (guy-**yeen**-ah) / hen

el gato / (**gah**-toh) / cat

el gatito / (gah-**tee**-toh) / small cat

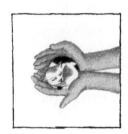

el gatitito / (gah-tee-**tee**-toh) / wee little cat

el gatititito / (gah-tee-tee-**tee**-toh) / super small cat

hasta luego / (**ah**-stah loo-**way**-go) / see you later

hola / (**oh**-la) / hello

los hombros / (**ohm**-brohz) / shoulders

hoy no va a estallar / (oy no vah a ess-tah-**yar**) / it's not going to explode today

la mano / (**mah**-noh) / hand

el mango / (**mahn**-goh) / mango

la mamá / (mah-**mah**) / mom

mucho gusto / (**moo**-cho **goo**-stow) /
   it's a pleasure to meet you

muy bien / (mwee bee-**yehn**) / very good

no sé, qué quieres hacer tú /
   (no say, kay kee-**ayr**-ays ah-**sayr** too) /
   I don't know, what do you want to do

la nariz / (nah-**rees**) / nose

no te preocupes / (no tay pray-oh-**koo**-payz) / don't worry

los ojos / (**oh**-hoze) / eyes

la paleta / (pah-**lay**-tah) / Popsicle

la paloma / (pah-**loh**-mah) / dove, pigeon

el papá / (pah-**pah**) / dad (if you say **pah**-pah, it means potato)

las patas / (**pah**-tahs) / animal legs

el pelo / (**pay**-loh) / hair

la pelota / (pay-**loh**-tah) / ball

el perro / (**pair**-oh) / dog

el perrito / (payr-**ee**-toh) / small dog

el perritito / (payr-ee-**tee**-toh) / wee little dog

el perrititito / (payr-ee-tee-**tee**-toh) / super small dog

el pez / (pehs) / fish (in the water)

el pescado / (pehs-**kah**-doh) / fish (out of the water)

las piernas / (pee-**yayr**-nah) / human legs

los pies / (pee-**yayz**) / feet

la playa subterránea / (**ply**-ah soob-teh-**rahn**-ay-ah) /
    underground beach

el pollo / (**poy**-yo) / young chicken or cooked chicken

las pulseras de la amistad / (pool-**sayr**-ahs day lah ah-mee-**stahd**) /
    friendship bracelets

la pupusa / (poo-**poo**-sah) / a thick tortilla with a filling

qué es / (kay ess) / what is (it)

qué es esto / (kay ess **ess**-toh) / what is this

qué tal, lagartija / (kay tahl, lah-gar-tee-ha) /
how's it going, little lizard

qué quieres hacer / (kay kee-**ayr**-ays ah-**sayr**) /
what do you want to do

quieres jugar / (kee-**ayr**-ays hoo-**gar**) / do you want to play

r-r-r-r-r-r-r-r / (d-d-d-d-d-d-d-d) / the sound of rolling Rs

la rana / (**rah**-nah) / frog

la rodilla / (roh-**dee**-yah) / knee

Simón dice / (see-**mohn dee**-say) / Simon Says

solo un poco / (**so**-loh oon **poh**-koh, oon rhymes with moon) / just
a little

somos amigas / (**soh**-mohs ah-**mee**-gahs) / we are friends (female)

somos amigos / (**soh**-mohs ah-**mee**-gohs) / we are friends (male,
or both male and female)

las sonrisas / (sohn-**ree**-sahs) / smiles

te lo prometo / (tay low pro-**may**-to) / I promise you

el tobillo / (toe-**bee**-yoh) / ankle

toca la cabeza / (**toe**-kah la kah-**bay**-sah) / touch your head

tuc tucs / (took-tooks, rhymes with books) /
   three-wheeled taxis

el trasero / (trah-**sayr**-oh) / rear end

el/la turista / (toor-**ees**-tah) / tourist

el volcán / (vol-**kahn**, vol rhymes with bowl) / volcano

la zorra / (**zorr**-ah) / female fox

el zorro / (**zorr**-oh) / male fox

And, in Kaqchikel:
la ütz awäch, ti spach / (la ootz ah-**wetch**, tee spahtch) /
   how's it going, little lizard